I0456814

MEMORY

& OTHER SHARDS

MEMORY

& OTHER SHARDS

(short stories)

Rachel Ige

WORDS
RHYMES &
RHYTHM

Printed and Published in Nigeria by:
Words Rhymes & Rhythm Limited
Suite C309, Global Plaza Plot 366, Obafemi
Awolowo Way, Jabi District, Abuja, Nigeria.
08169027757, 08060109295
www.wrr.ng

CONTENTS

DEDICATION

To Àísá and Remi, watch the ocean ripple!

"CONCOBILITY"

When I think of a perfect date, the only thing that comes to mind is the man and the attraction between us. Tonight, the man who led me down to our reserved seat, was the real deal - handsome, capable, confident and sought by many. I wasn't lacking in anyway either; I looked good and didn't need a mirror to know that. The multitude of eyes plastered on us as we walked in was enough pointer. I had taken my time to pick out the dress I was wearing.

To me, simplicity was a necessity. I didn't want to wear anything that would fixate his eyes on my body, whilst ogling it, neither did I appreciate the plaid look. Alluring yet sensible was just the description for my short-sleeved long lacy yellow gown, which was complemented by my black purse and pumps.

When we reached our table, my date briefly dropped my hand to pull back my chair. I sat down regally and straightened my back. I thought to myself,

Nothing must go wrong with this date.

Smiling, I looked at the young handsome man who sat before me - Mr.Bayo Yolanda-Cole, one of those Badagry-based boys, with an undeniable *tushness*. Mr. Cole happened to be the only son of the Chief

Executive Officer of Darryl Communication Ltd, a telecommunication company where I worked as the Human Resource manager. Rumours had spread about the CEO's adorable and brilliant son, who bagged a first class degreein law from Harvard University. It had been a year since I begun working at Darryl yet I had never caught a glimpse of him until recently.

Tonight, however, I had an eyeful as I sat across the table one-on-one with this dashing gentleman, admiring his silky blue shirt complemented by a black suede jacket. The gold chain hanging around his neck was too shiny for me but heck, I could cope with a little glitch. Mr. Cole snapped his fingers and a waiter came at once. He picked a delicacy from the menu for both of us, and asked that it be accompanied by a bottle of vintage red wine.

I was a little displeased that he didn't ask for my preference and just assumed that I would take whatever he ordered. Ignoring my preference was not really the crux of the issue but only a symptom. A symptom of the perilous archaic dismissal of the female clime and their opinions, and the ridiculous view that every woman is a damsel that must be rescued from distress. If I was a man, Mr. Cole would have asked me for my preference or better still left me to order my own dish.

Ordinarily, I would have let him know without mincing words how inappropriate that was but tonight, I was in a good mood as the memory of earlier events of the day was still dancing in my head.

Just forgive him.

"Mr. Cole, I just want to thank you for inviting me over for dinner. It's really been wonderful so far." I rambled nervously.

My date chuckled.

"Please, call me Baycole, all my friends call me that...and you haven't seen nothing,"

He winked at that last statement and my suspicious alter ego reared up her head, speaking softly in my mind.

What does he mean by that?

Before I could think further, our food arrived, and the waiter placed it gently on our table. I looked at the appetizing meal of rich jollof rice slathered with coleslaw and a considerably weighty piece of chicken wings. Then I noticed the cutlery,

Great! It's fork and knife.

I smirked at my own sarcasm-laced thoughts. Although I could effortlessly eat with a fork and knife, I rarely did. For me, it was too bougie and gratuitous but for a place like this, I could keep up appearances. With my back ramrod straight, I picked up my cutlery and started to eat. I did not know that Baycole was watching until I heard his sigh of satisfaction.

Really? I asked myself incredulously. So he thought I couldn't wield the fork and knife? How funny.

I continued eating and took great pains making him think I was unaware of his stares. He started eating too and for about five minutes, there were no words spoken, just occasional clangs made whenever our cutlery slightly grazed our plates.

"So, Mildred..."

Briefly startled, I raised my head and faced the man who just called my name. Baycole was still smiling at me when he continued,"What do you like about me? Why did you agree to dine with me?" he asked.

Okay, Mr. Badagry has already concluded that I like him because I agreed to go on one date. One!

Maybe I was just misinterpreting his questions. The man could just be wondering why he got a "yes" on his first trial, despite the rebuffs I had given several colleagues. I decided to indulge him.

"Well, ask and it shall be given," I chuckled at my own light joke before continuing. "I just wanted a chance to know you better, beyond the rumours,"

"What rumours?"His voice was slightly curious.

I struggled unsuccessfully to insert vagueness into my reply. "Errm...well, that you bagged a first class degree in law at a Harvard...that you have a very unique taste,"

He eased back and smiled smugly."I guess you have confirmed those rumours,"

At this point, I began to wonder if his confidence was not teetering on the edge of pride. However, I could not argue with his delicate taste. The restaurant, which we were dining in, was well furbished, with everything being state-of-the-art; even the food he picked out had an exquisite taste.

We continued eating while he tried to sustain the conversation.

"What are the qualities you would love to have in a, errr...partner?"

What's with all these personal questions? Is he taking this thing seriously?

I took great care and time in chewing and swallowing the food in my mouth. I wouldn't want to spray him with half-chewed rice when speaking. Calmly, while avoiding the bottle of red wine, I poured water into my glass cup and took a few sips. Then I answered. I had so many preferred qualities but I didn't want to appear vain, so I told him the fundamental ones.

"Well, I'd like my man to be a Christian, to be truthful and humble, with a kind heart,"

He was nodding.

"What about you? What do you like about me?" I asked.

"Your English,"

I wasn't prepared for his answer and I just stared unblinkingly.

"Seriously?"

"Yeah seriously. You see, I listened to your acceptance speech today and your diction was perfect, and the words used? Impeccable. Plus you had no local accent, you may have well been Julia Roberts."

Yes, I remember my acceptance speech. Earlier today, at the company's end of the year luncheon, I had been awarded "The Best Employee of the Year". I was so happy that I had grinned and grinned for hours. Who wouldn't if they had a substantial amount of money attached to that award? I just said some words of gratitude; I couldn't even remember them now.

Still staring incredulously, I asked; "Is that all?"

"You mean asides your beautiful skin and *ajebota* deluxe body? Yeah, that's all."

His eyes were still roving with a smirk on his lips as he continued,"You see, I like a bold, daring and classy woman, someone who I can easily introduce to my friends without fear or shame; not a local girl that taints her tongue with local languages. I once took a girl out to a dinner like this, although my friends were there also. Her mother called her phone and she picked up and said, "Hello maami". Maami! Like who says that anymore? I was so red to the roots with shame. At a point, I couldn't take it anymore. I picked my keys, walked out to my car and drove away. I never called her again..."

My mind was in space as Baycole rambled on. Of course, I could speak English fluently and had an arsenal of seasoned and gigantic words that most have never heard. This could be attributed to my voracious reading of any and every thing that contained words. Yet, I knew my roots were important, that African culture was fading, being washed out by westernisation and our local languages were being sunk beneath an ocean of colonisation.

Our identity has been compromised and soon enough, our origin would be lost. Bearing this in mind, I had made up my mind to appreciate culture, ensure and encourage people (especially Yorubas) to speak their language and disgraced anyone who felt that I was unrefined for speaking my mother tongue. Baycole was still talking.

"...since then, I always make sure that any girl I'm interested in can speak English. In fact, I feel better if she doesn't even have any acquaintance with these barbaric tongues."

Yoruba? Barbaric?

My mind was already busy spinning. What can I do to teach this man a lesson? He was obviously a twit so merely voicing my disagreement will not cut it. I already had a plan in mind. Across the bar, some feet away from us, a lady was being disturbed by another young man's unwanted advances. The lady, obviously trying to avoid a commotion, just kept turning away. I smiled mischievously.

He doesn't like embarrassment, abi?

Calmly, I interrupted Baycole. "Excuse me, I need to attend to certain matters." He nodded assent.

Still seated, I raised my voice at the rancorous "gentleman".

"Bros, leave that girl nah. She say she no do, abi nah by force? Carry your wahaladey go, abeg!"

Baycole's eyes were round with shock as he listened to my Pidgin English.

Ooh! I was enjoying this.

Gently, I leaned forward, smiling demurely as I whispered; *"O ya e lenu abi? Wón ní omo alé ló n fi owó òsì júwe Ilé baba rè.* Guess what that makes you?"

By then, everyone's attention had been diverted to our table.

I stood up and spoke to Baycole, just loud enough for everyone around to hear. I also ensured that my words were impeccable and my Queen's English, flawless.

"Now listen to me, Mr Bayonle Cole," I ensured that the right Yoruba indentation on the "Bayonle" was well pronounced. "Not only do I find your words demeaning and degrading, I also consider them as insulting to the African race in general. Your shiny credentials and blings..." My middle and forefingers on both hands bent and wiggled, to accentuate a quote on the word 'blings'. "do not entitle you to throw shades at your culture. People like you are murderers, who are inhumanely and slowly snuffing the life out of your culture, and all for what? A westernisation you would never be truly considered a part of? Yoruba, barbaric? You make me sick!"

With that, I snatched my purse and flounced, fuming out of the restaurant. Just at the exit, I risked a brief glance back at the table and what I saw brought a smile of satisfaction to my lips. Baycole's jaw was still droopy.

Just like my chances of still being employed by tomorrow, I thought wryly.

I knew I would wake up with regrets the next day but his expression of shock and the whole room casting accusatory glances at him, kept me warm that night.

I smiled and hailed a cab.

"Only a bastard points at his father's house with his left hand."

Concobility- A slang for "nonsense".

RANTINGS OF INSANITY

It didn't matter who was watching, because I did not even care. They had a lot to look at and as a matter of fact I would stare unabashed if I were in their shoes.

It was at this moment I doubted my sanity, it's funny though, because I never once thought I was crazy, not when I kissed a statue fully on the mouth, putting my tongue in her stony mouth during an excursion to the museum during my secondary school days, or when I received a phone-call right in front of lecturers and others while defending a project in one of my courses (Of course, I failed that course), not even few minutes ago when I ran out of my house in just my oversized shirt with no underwear below the belt and my hair covered in soap sods did I think I was crazy.

I was wondering if I should take a cab to my destination and made an attempt to retrieve money from my non-existent trousers, it was then it registered that I wasn't wearing any. This effort of mine revealed my private part for all to see. I saw several school girls bashfully turn their faces away and carefully sneak a peek when they thought no one was paying attention to them. I watched adults sadly wag their heads. Well if they knew why I was in this state, they would be cheering me on because I was on a mission to save the world and I had just six hours to get to Sokoto state and since no one was willing to give me a ride, I gladly walked. Ibadan could not be that far from Sokoto.

Hehe! I know you are curious about what danger the world was in and how I could help avert the impending disaster. I am seriously contemplating telling you, I just don't know if EYEFUNMI would mind if I told you.

Who is Eyefunmi?

She was my great grandmother. She died 50 years before I was born and I still know her, isn't that great?

Well, she and I had been in communication ever since I was seven when she told me in a dream that I had a father and a mother, and that they loved me so much regardless of anything that happened. I was surprised to see her in my dream, however, ever since then; I had always tried to do whatever she asked me to do.

I was just bathing some minutes ago preparing for a job interview when she appeared to me again. By the way, I graduated with a first class honors from the Department of Psychology in the University of Ibadan.

In an urgent voice, Eyefunmi told me that Obatala and Ogun were angry with mortals and wanted their bloods to flow. She said even Esu felt like he stank and needed a bloodbath and so that was why he instigated Boko Haram into violence by planting a mustard seed into the sandy heart of Sokoto dunes. She added that the only way to redeem mankind was to get the seed out of the sands. And that was exactly what I was on my way to do.

All of a sudden, I feel two strong men grab me, one clamped me hard on the shoulders and the other held me tight around the stomach. I look around wildly. Oh my God! They must think I am mad.

Ah!!! They do not know my story. Tell them....tell them the future of mankind depends on me, tell them I am not mad... or am I mad?

FATE: MEMORIES GAVE ME CHILLS

Fate, they say is inescapable. I'm not an ardent believer in destiny; I believe that man makes or mars himself. However, once in a while, Oogway's words in the animation movie, Kong Fu Panda, waft into my ears.

"One often meets his destiny on the path to avoiding it."

Then I'm reminded of Odewale and his cursed destiny in Wole Rotimi's "The Gods are not to Blame". Most of all, I'm reminded of that fateful day.

I still get chills anytime I remember. The sun aglow on that day and the air was warm but I still got chills. My freshman year was filled with toil, turmoil and a dash of confusion. As law students, every day we moved from one department to the other like a herd of nomadic cows wandering for grass.

That day was no different, however, we had just finished our final class for the day at Faculty of Arts; Philosophy 101 (Philosophy and Mankind). The course that taught that since God doesn't appeal to any of your five senses, then He most definitely doesn't exist and the lecturers make so much sense while at it. Now that I think of it, I realize that the sixth sense was not put into play. Yes, that inexplicable sense we call instincts or guts. The existence of a supreme being directing the affairs on earth appeal to that sense.

After that class, my classmates and I walked back to our hostels. As we trod out of the faculty, everywhere was abuzz with people talking in groups. The sun was setting and I never liked to walk alone when it does. So, I attached myself to a group of females walking to my hostel, Queen Idia Hall. I was flanked on both sides by two students even as we walked on a row. There was a lot of chatter going on around me but I was quiet. I had just being taught a lesson in class that challenged the crux of my belief and religion and it was too bitter a pill to swallow. That, coupled with the fact that I had to "think-walk", made me fall in step with my classmates and occupy my mind with something less disturbing.

At that point, we had reached the confluence of business and 'busy-ness'; SUB (The Students Union Building). Though situated a few metres away from where we walked, the building was popular enough to force its name on its environs. There were several people sparsely distributed, hooting at passers-by; "Typing, photocopy, printing, passport...." With the exception of a few restaurants, snack-selling shops and a little garage filled with some cabs, the bulk of the services rendered at SUB were clerical in nature.

We had barely reached the net-cordoned area of the lawny tennis court when a large hand grabbed my arm. Instantly, I turned to have a look at the person who grabbed me, thinking it must be a friend who could barely contain his/her excitement, or who was merely trying to be mischievous.

It turned out to be neither. The person holding my arm was a man, a huge one in a blue and red coloured sports jacket worn with faded brown trousers. He seemed to be double my height and much more in size. I looked at his enormous boots and my gaze travelled to his face. My heart quickened in fear. He was not wearing a frown, neither was he scowling. It was his wide-toothed grin that made shivers crawl up my spine and my heart melt into a puddle.

His bearded face was like a bush of thorns cradling a huge ostrich's egg. I tried to jerk my arm away but his grip was vice-like. I looked around wildly and no one seemed interested, everyone walked along straight-faced. Couldn't they see us? Couldn't they see my panic?

My classmates had walked on; none of them was looking back. Oddly, I didn't even think to scream. I was still twisting my arms with little or no result in getting away. I turned my face to my assailant with the intention of requesting a release. Only then did he speak just once with his gaze on mine, unwavering. I was expecting a booming voice in proportion to his size but his voice was almost soft. He spoke once, just once and his words were simple but their effects, chilly.

"You have been noticed."

At the sound of his voice, the spell seemed to break. I jerked again and my arms came free. Without thinking, I ran and didn't look back. As my legs lifted one after the other, the voice reverberated in my head.

"You have been noticed."

"You have been noticed."

I wanted to scream out my confusion. Who? Who noticed me? Why? What have I done?

I ran until I reached my deserting classmates who didn't notice that I was missing until I rejoined them. "What happened? Where were you?" I realized that none of them saw what just happened, so I kept mum. I didn't answer their questions. I only folded my arms across my breasts, my shivering hands stroking them in the dwindling heat.

When I got to the hostel, I narrated my experience to a friend. Her raised eyebrows spiked up my fear, but the words that followed calmed me a little.

"Oh, you met him? He isn't alright." she raised her index finger up to her temple while the other fingers remained bunched into a fist and rotated it to signify mental instability. "That's how he grabs girls anyhow. He grabbed me once too."

Still, I could not help but wonder.

Why me? We were five on a row, I was not even at the edge. Why was I singled out? I could have been hurt right amidst the throng and no one would notice.

Right from that day however, anytime I hear the sentence; "There is safety in numbers", I just scoff and mutter to myself, "Only, only if danger has got someone else on his hit-list."

TERROR

For those whose senses died, and those whose body followed suit,
What kills is not on the battlefield, its lies right in our homes.

Sophie just lay there, immobile on the bed and allowed Ken to do whatever he pleased with her body. She wasn't in the mood for sex, but what could she do? It was his conjugal right, and she could not deprive him of it. "Tell him," her mind whispered to her, but she quickly dispelled the thought. The last time she had tried giving a hint by her actions, he....

She shut her eyes deeply, willing herself not to remember. But the images, vivid ones, flooded her mind. Her husband had thrown her on the floor, ripped her clothes off, and after series of hurtful jabs and smacks; availed himself of his sexual lust despite all the signs which signified that she wasn't ready for the penile invasion.

He was doing it again now. The last time he tried to rape her and she struggled, she couldn't walk for days. Bruises were all over her vagina, she had to seek medical attention. Of course, she lied that she got the bruises from roughly fixing her tampons. So she laid there, tears running down her eyes, but they didn't stay on her cheek for long, as her husband kissed her and licked up her tears.

It was not the first time. But, tonight's incidence stirred a well of brooding water in Sophie. The water twirled and swirled until it matched the pace of an erupting volcano. She was no longer in control of her mind, and it felt good to be in that state. Calmly, she ran her hands through her hair, searching, until she found it. With all the strength she could muster, and with a crazy banshee scream, she plunged deep. She watched his eyes go round with shock, until he collapsed right atop her.

Sophie did not move, all she did was take labored heaves of breath.

Occasionally, her husband's head lifted along with her chest when she breathed deeply. She closed her eyes and went to sleep. And that was how the police found her sleeping with her husband's lifeless body astride her, a metal hair pin stuck to his neck. At first, they thought that she was dead too, for how could one person spill that much blood? It was just too much. What baffled the Inspector was Sophie's calm smile, looking back at her husband's dead body whilst being whisked away. It gave him chills.

Her lawyer pled insanity, but Sophie had never felt more sane. The judge accepted, regardless of provocation, the actions of the accused after the murder proved that she indeed had had a "visitation of God". He pitifully ordered her to be incarcerated, with close observation in a psychiatric hospital. She felt serenely safe on this brink of insanity. Every time, whenever she was not being attended to by the doctor, she laid in the same position with her back flat on the bed, and her two hands cradling her head. The nurses saw it as a peaceful state; she knew it was a precautionary one. Just in case the ghost of her husband came back, she routinely strokes the pin with which she held her hair.

FEAR

Cold sweat ran down the goose bumps on his skin. Terrified beyond measures, he felt rather than saw the four pairs of little fingers clutching at his long kaftan, they were the hands of his children. His wife tried to maintain some form of nobility, in order to forestall the chaos that was threatening to burst out in the silence, but the terror in her eyes was loud enough for him to see. It seemed like they were screaming, with silent words; "Are we going to die?"

He had just received a call; this call put a stop to the air of festivity in the house. Even the bolus of Tuwo got stuck in his throat as the saliva meant to push it down, dried up instantly. Seeing the look of apprehension on his face, his wife put off the radio, ceasing the loud music that blared from it, leaving the whining voices of the ignorant kids as the only sign of life in the house and stared with bulging eyes.

"Alhaji, what is it?"

Still holding the phone inches away from his left ear like a dangling wrap of explosives which might explode anytime soon, Abdul rahman blurted out in shock, "Thieves."

Balqis, a woman of frail form, thin to the extent that when she walked, it was feared that she could break or get carried away by the wind. Her husband, Abdul, as he was often called by friends never allowed her go out in a storm. It was still a source of amazement in the community how she managed to give birth to four children and still stayed alive. When she heard the stunning word "thieves" from her husband's mouth, her face grew so ashen such that one would conclude that even if the rigours of childbirth did not kill her, this news was sure to do the job. She whispered in fear to her husband; "They are going to kill us."

"Ahusubilahi,"[1] he replied in short reprimand, but his voice betrayed him and revealed that he had the same fear.

Early that morning, his joy knew no bounds when the juicy contract which he had been after for some months now bounced into his laps. Of course, he had to be very happy, who wouldn't be happy if they got a government contract of five million naira when the expense was not more than two million naira? And to top it, forty percent of the money was paid up front with a promise of paying the remaining percent when the contract has been executed. Stealthily, Abdul had carried duffel bags containing three million naira to his house. He should have deposited the money into his bank account

---

[1] God forbid.

but he just wanted to dazzle Balqis, which was why he insisted on being paid in cash. Besides it was eight o' clock in the evening, banks had closed already.

"I'll make sure that by nine tomorrow morning; I get to the bank, what harm would ten hours of staying in a house do to the money? Who would suspect that I can harbour such amount of money in my humble house?" he had thought to himself.

Indeed, Abdul rahman's house was more than humble; it was humbling. The walls were unplastered with crayon paintings at every turn. Of course, the children made sure that if their father knew little or nothing about decoration they would lend him helping hands. So they scribbled writings on the wall. Iqbal, the youngest who was about three years old, drew Mickey mouse (at least, that was what he called it). The pathetic mosaic on the wall resembled Gandhi's gnarled form rather than the cheeky Mickey mouse. All these chased away the thoughts of ever been robbed from Abdul's mind.

Now it was happening, or would be happening in a few minutes. His neighbour who also happened to be his friend had just called to notify him of the four masked men who seem to be walking towards the direction of his house. His neighbour had seen this with the aid of CCTV cameras and many other facilities that helped him spy on the night workers of theft.

Abdul moved to the window side in a bid to close it, but Balqis, thinking it was an attempt to run away spoke in a broken voice. "Alhaji, are you running away?"

On hearing that question, Suleiman, the eldest of Abdul's children clung to his father's kaftan, making the others follow suit. This marked the birth of a ridiculous situation, four childish hands holding onto their father's cloth with beseeching eyes.

Seeing that there was nothing to be done, the family sat down on the rug cross-legged, joining hands together like a band of shamans praying for the peace of the clan, waiting for that dreaded bang of a gun. The whole family started to ask for forgiveness from God. Even if we die, we will die praying and claiming our rewards, thought Balqis. And so the family started to beg for pardon, chanting "Astargafurulahi".[2]

What they heard was a knock; the first rap of knuckles on the door caused Abdul's eyebrow to rise in utmost show of surprise. Since when did robbers start knocking politely on doors? He looked at his wife whose careful shrug indicated that anything was possible in this country called Nigeria. As a result, none but Abdul who had not been praying wholeheartedly, but being

---

[2] A prayer for forgiveness

worried about the three million naira stashed in his wardrobe, heard the loud protest of the door as it was kicked down and stomped hard, raising dust off the floor. He turned to see the gun pointed at him, immediately he shut his eyes and screamed;

"The money is in the wardrobe walahi!"

"And where are the robbers?" was the reply.

"Please don't shoot m..." he paused midway as the realization of what he heard just sank in. Carefully, he cracked one eye open and timidly stuttered; "The...the robbers..?"

Lowering his gun, the black uniformed man put his hand into his shirt to bring out something and Abdul quickly shut his eyes again thinking; "Oh God, not a bomb, ah! Why will these wasteful fellows want to destroy all that money with a bomb, it is better if they carry it sef, chai! I'll be unidentifiable when this is all over."

Seconds ticked by and there was no loud roaring of fire, not even a single boom, it was a nudge from his wife that made him open his eyes again to see the police badge stretched at him. "I am Inspector Duru from Bayero division, Sango. We got a call about a probable robbery attack on you and family; I guess it was just a prank call, we are sorry to disturb your peace."

Abdul rahman just stared, his mouth shaped in a silent "o". The expression on his face was one of utmost surprise, then gradually it transcended into that of relief, then anger; white fury.

"What is wrong with all these rich paranoid people? Look at this man raising a false alarm, he didn't even allow me to finish my Tuwo." Abdulrahman said while thinking of the cranky call his neighbour made to him to deliver the 'now false' news. The family watched the band of policemen slowly walk out through the non-existent door.

For Abdul rahman that night, sleep was a 'utopic' dream. After tucking his children to sleep, he sat down with eyes wide and unblinking. By morning, his erstwhile white eyeball had acquired a hue of red and even before 6:00 am Abdul was out of his house, in his car, speeding to the bank, leaving dust to settle behind.

MY DIARY, MY BEST FRIEND

With a sigh of exasperation I dropped the fork and knife in my hands, and did a survey of my body. Well before I did that, I noticed the scraps of food on the floor; precious grains of rice littered the cold cement of my room. If my mum had the opportunity to view this, she would raise her hands in astonishment and ask why in heaven I was eating like a rat, my mother always used funny comparisons. Then, my eyes strayed to the top I was wearing and I wondered why I was refused the job of an art teacher which I applied for in a remote secondary school, because the mosaic painting I just finished making on my shirt, would make Van Ghog jealous.

That was when the tears dropped from my eyes and then I realized that I couldn't just do this. Do what exactly? I thought back to the question that brought this misery into my life;

".....would you go with me?"

I just couldn't think that Llyod would ask me, despite the abundance of cool sophisticated girls in the faculty to go out with him and be his date to the faculty of Law dinner which would be starting in the next thirty minutes. It wasn't as if I was ugly,

I had a lot of "wooers" most of them were from my faculty which was why they didn't count to me.

I am a 200 level student of Theatre Arts, fair, and averagely tall with a curvy shape that most guys would call sexy. As a matter of fact, I get a lot of such sassy comments from those randy boys during their infamous "aro" anytime I pass through on the way to my hostel. I'm an Idiaite by the way though I live at Agbowo now. Sometimes I just go along with them and smile shyly, and sometimes I just walk on with a deadpan expression on my face. It all depends on my mood. And then I just wonder, 'what if I was wearing trousers? Means those guys would go comatose'. Yes, I never wear trousers due to rules of my denomination, but anytime I'm asked why, I'll just simply say I don't want to be an object of lust because I've got wide and very round hips. With all these, I'm sure you are wondering why the excitement over a guy asking me out. I'll tell you more about Llyod and then maybe you would understand.

Llyod Kago is a 400 level law student, awesomely tall and dark in complexion. He possessed pink lips that always appeared moist anytime I see him. I have always been attracted to dark guys right from the start. Wait! Here is the catch; currently, he is the president of the Law Students Association and his name has always appeared on the

Dean's honour list since his admission into the school. Well, that wasn't really what made him attractive to me. I guess it was the way he walked modestly without noticing the aura that he oozed. When I interacted with him and I discovered that he was a Christian, I mean a real Christian, not the fake ones that hide behind the Bible and prophetic anointing; I feel I can safely say I have a crush on him.

I know girls would know how I feel, I mean that weird sense of euphoria you get when a secret crush of yours asks you out on a date. I just couldn't think straight for days, I found myself avoiding the company of my friends so I could have some private, quality time to think about the glorious expression on his face while uttering those wonderful words. Well, I don't think I would be attending the dinner with him, and since I could not muster the courage to tell him, I sent a text to him to that effect. Then I sat down on the floor, back against the wall, legs humped forward with my head lolled forward, resting on them. It was in this state that Llyod found me. I didn't even know when he entered the room, and yet, when I felt a weight settle down on the floor beside me, I knew it was him without raising my head, the scent of his perfume betrayed him.

"I got your text message, why? You don't want to go with me? Or you have another date?" I looked up with a tears-stained face in time to see his oesophagus bubbling in an awkward swallow. I slowly shook my head, and said tearfully; "Lloyd I am sorry but I can't afford to embarrass you, I don't know how to eat with fork and knife."

He heaved a sigh of relief and just put his arms around me, and that was how we stayed till late at night, dinner forgotten, with no cares except for ourselves. Not a word was said except a kiss on the forehead when he was leaving for home. He was a gentleman.

"He is still a gentleman." I said to myself, smiling as I read the last words of the diary I kept when I was in university. "Honey I'm off to work, I'll pick the kids from school, love you." I heard my husband yell from the doorway. I closed the diary that I was reading from and smiled.

"I love you too, Mr Kago."

It is fun keeping diaries.

PROFILE

Ige Rachel is a graduate of the University of Ibadan. She writes short stories and poems and has had some of her works featured on platforms like *FFM*, *TheNakedConvos*, etc, and in anthologies like "Uites Write", "October Stories" and "Epistles of Lies". She has won prizes in Poetry contests like the Brigitte Poirson Poetry Contest 2017 (May edition), Scribble the Future Poetry contest, and Okigbo poetry competition. She was also a finalist in the Ego Aghedo Poetry competition 2013. Memory and Other Shards is her first book. She is currently studying at the Nigerian Law School, Abuja.